The Berenstain Bears

Do the Right Thing

"Fight the good fight, holding
on to faith and a good conscience."

—1 Timothy 1:18, 19

ZONDERKIDZ

The Berenstain Bears® Do the Right Thing
Copyright © 2019 by Berenstain Publishing, Inc.
Illustrations © 2019 by Berenstain Publishing, Inc.

Requests for information should be addressed to:
Zonderkidz, 3900 *Sparks Dr. SE, Grand Rapids, Michigan 49546*

ISBN 978-0-310-76362-8

Editor: Annette Bourland
Design: Cindy Davis

Printed in the United States of America.

19 20 CWM 10 9 8 7 6 5 4 3 2

By Mike Berenstain
Based on the characters created by
Stan & Jan Berenstain

Living Lights™

A Faith Story

ZONDERkidz

Bear Town Park was a popular place and a happy place. It was always full of cubs playing on seesaws and slides, batting a ball around, or just hanging out with their friends.

Sister and Brother were headed for the park one lazy Saturday afternoon. They had their baseball bats and gloves, and Sister had a backpack full of her favorite Beary Buddy dolls. She collected them and hoped her friends would be in the park with their dolls too.

At the park, Sister spotted a group of Beary Buddy collectors and made a beeline for them.

"Hey, Sister!" someone called from the baseball field. It was Cousin Fred. "Come join our game. We need a shortstop."

"Yes," agreed Brother. "We need you on our team."

"Sister!" the other players cried. "Sister! Sister!"

Sister liked Beary Buddies. But she liked baseball too. Besides, she was flattered that everyone wanted her to play. She made up her mind. Baseball, it was.

Sister played a fine game that afternoon. She was a talented shortstop and made some terrific plays.

When the game was over, though, her mind turned to thoughts of Beary Buddies.

She looked around for her collector friends but they were gone. She could see them in the distance, heading for home.

Disappointed, Sister turned back to the ballfield. But she noticed something lying under a bush.

Pushing the leaves aside she found … a *Beary Buddy!*

It was Chub Cub—a very special doll that was hard to come by. Someone must have lost it—probably Sister's friend, Millie, who had a Chub Cub in her collection. Millie would be upset when she found the doll missing. Sister thought of running after her friends. But they were long gone. She looked at the little Chub Cub doll. It was adorable!

Brother noticed Sister picking up the doll. He wondered what she was up to.

"Sister!" he called. "We need to go home for dinner now."

Sister didn't know what to do about the lost Chub Cub. It probably did belong to Millie. But she wasn't there and Sister had to go home to dinner.

"Oh, well," she told Chub Cub. "I'll think about that tomorrow." She slipped the doll into her backpack with the rest of her Beary Buddies and joined Brother.

After dinner, Sister and Honey played with Beary Buddies in the living room. Brother was reading nearby. The dolls were having a tea party to welcome Chub Cub to their group.

"So nice of you to join us, Chub Cub!" Sister said, pretending to be Foozle Fur, her favorite.

"Thank you so much!" said Honey, pretending to be Chub Cub.

Chub Cub seemed happy in his new home. In fact, Sister was already thinking of him as part of her collection. He fit in so well.

"Chub Cub?" said Brother, looking up. He knew a thing or two about Beary Buddies. "I didn't know you had a Chub Cub. I hear they're hard to find. Everyone wants one. Aren't you the lucky one!"

Hmm, Sister thought. *Was she the lucky one?* She wondered how Millie would feel about that. It made her a little uncomfortable.

"Brother," she said, "can I ask you a question?"

"Sure, Sis," said Brother, reading.

"Suppose someone found something in the park that was very special," said Sister. "Would it be okay to keep it?"

Brother looked up.

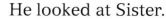

He looked at Sister.

He looked at Chub Cub.

"I don't think so," said Brother. "When you find something valuable, like money or jewelry, you're supposed to give it to a lost-and-found or the police or someone like that. Then whoever lost it can get it back."

"Oh," said Sister. She looked at Chub Cub and sighed.

"Brother," said Sister.

"What?" asked Brother, closing his book.

"How do you know what's right or what's wrong if you're not really sure?" she wondered.

"You've got to let your conscience be your guide," said Brother.

"My conscience?" asked Sister. She had heard about 'conscience' but wasn't sure what it was.

"Your conscience is like a small voice inside your head that tells you to do the right thing," Brother explained.

The idea of a small voice inside her head seemed weird to Sister and she looked worried.

"Just pretend you've got a little angel sitting on your shoulder," suggested Brother. "Then, when you're not sure what to do, you can ask the angel and the angel will whisper the answer in your ear."

Sister liked that idea. She imagined an angel in a long yellow nightie sitting on her shoulder. She thought of a question.

"What do you think I should do?" she asked the angel, quietly in her mind.

"You must do the right thing!" the angel answered. "Return Chub Cub to his rightful owner!"

"Okay," said Sister, relieved. "I will. And I'll always let my conscience be my guide."

The next day, Sister returned to the park where she found her friends with their Beary Buddies.

"Did anyone lose a Chub Cub?" she asked, taking it out of her backpack.

"My Chub Cub!" said Millie. "I've been looking for him everywhere!
I was so worried!" She took the doll and hugged it happily.

Then Millie gave Sister a big hug too. "Thank you, Sister!" she cried. "It was so nice of you to bring him back."

That made Sister feel good. She had been worried she would be sad about giving up Chub Cub. But she wasn't sad at all. She was happy. Letting your conscience be your guide turned out to be a pretty good deal.

"Thanks!" Sister said to the imaginary angel on her shoulder.

"No," said Millie, overhearing her, "thank you!"

"You're welcome!" said Sister with a big smile. And the angel on her shoulder smiled back with pride.